W9-CPD-192

Coldwater Public Library, Coldwater, Ohio

FERNANDO KRAHN

The Secret in the Dungeon

CLARION BOOKS/TICKNOR & FIELDS: A HOUGHTON MIFFLIN COMPANY/NEW YORK

Clarion Books
Ticknor & Fields, a Houghton Mifflin Company

Copyright © 1983 by Fernando Krahn
All rights reserved. No part of this work may be reproduced
or transmitted in any form or by any means, electronic or
mechanical, including photocopying and recording, or by any
information storage or retrieval system, except as may be
expressly permitted by the 1976 Copyright Act or in writing
by the publisher. Requests for permission should be addressed
in writing to Clarion Books, 52 Vanderbilt Avenue, New York, NY 10017.

Printed in the U.S.A.

Library of Congress Cataloging in Publication Data
Krahn, Fernando.
The secret in the dungeon.
Summary: A curious child slips away from
a tour group at an old castle and stumbles
upon a sleeping dragon in a dungeon.
[1. Dragons—Fiction.   2. Stories without words]   I. Title.
PZ7.K8585Sde   1983   [E]   82-9595
ISBN 0-89919-148-7

Y 10 9 8 7 6 5 4 3 2 1

Dday
9/1/1983
9.95

MEDIEVAL
CASTLE

58272

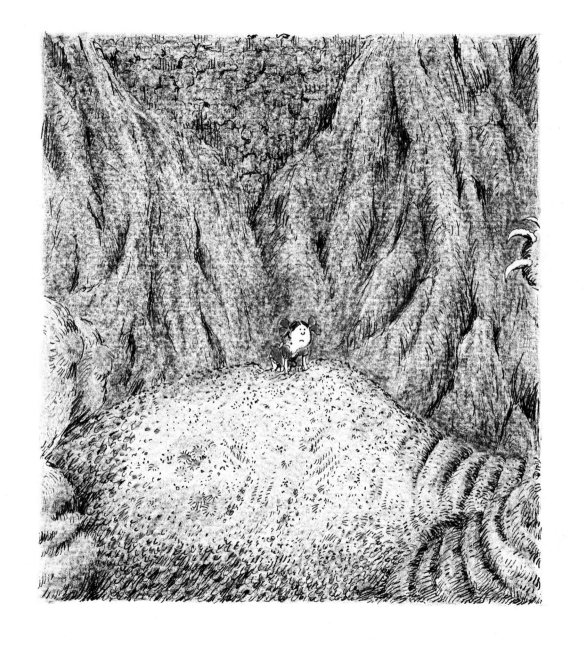

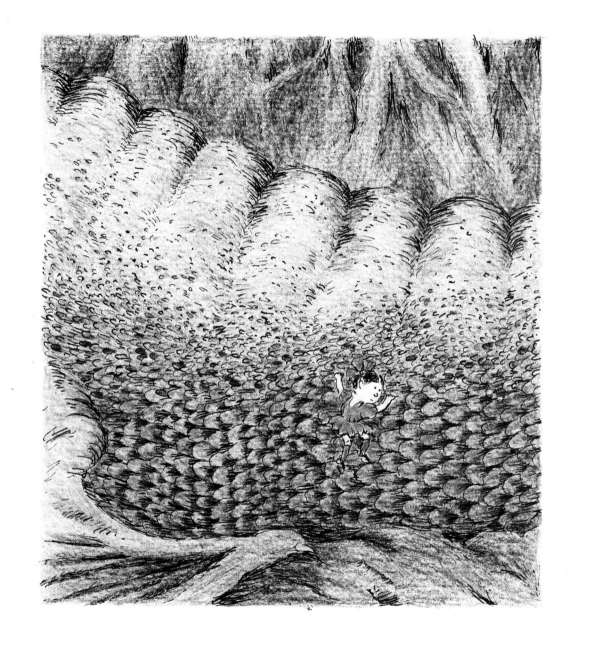

Coldwater Public Library, Coldwater, Ohio

58272